The saucer was very well hidden. . . .

It was so black that it seemed to blend in with the night and the darkness.

The spaceship was also big, bigger than I'd thought when it first sailed overhead. It was as big as a circus tent, but not nearly as tall—more like an enormous Frisbee.

There was a soft swooshing noise from the saucer . . . and a set of steps slid out onto the ground, landing with a light thud.

There was a soft glow from inside, and we could see the dark silhouette of someone—or something—standing in the doorway.

"It's a space alien!" the Big T screeched.

Books by Bill Crider

Mike Gonzo and the Sewer Monster
Mike Gonzo and the Almost Invisible Man
Mike Gonzo and the UFO Terror

Available from MINSTREL Books

Mike GONZO and the UFO Terror

BILL CRIDER

A MINSTREL® BOOK

Published by POCKET BOOKS
New York   London   Toronto   Sydney   Tokyo   Singapore

This book is a work of fiction. Names, characters, places and
incidents are products of the author's imagination or are used
fictitiously. Any resemblance to actual events or locales or
persons, living or dead, is entirely coincidental.

A MINSTREL PAPERBACK *Original*

A Minstrel Book published by
POCKET BOOKS, a division of Simon & Schuster Inc.
1230 Avenue of the Americas, New York, NY 10020

ISBN: 0-671-53653-2

First Minstrel Books printing January 1997

10 9 8 7 6 5 4 3 2 1

A MINSTREL BOOK and colophon are registered trademarks of
Simon & Schuster Inc.

Cover art by Broeck Steadman

Printed in the U.S.A.

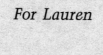

For Lauren

Mike GONZO and the UFO Terror

Chapter 1

Unidentified Flying Object

The first person in Midgeville to be abducted by a UFO was Jimmy Terwilliger.

The way Jimmy told it, two days ago he'd been walking through the parking lot at one of the Midgeville baseball fields. A Little League team had played a game there that evening, and Jimmy had hung around afterward to look for money under the stands.

He found two quarters, a dime, and a penny; then he started home. He got about halfway to his street before he saw the lights. When he looked up into the ring of brightness, he heard a sound that he said "was a little like a vacuum cleaner."

1

Bill Crider

He started to yell, and then he was sucked up into the sky, right into some kind of spaceship, where some strange little creatures poked and prodded him with funny-looking implements that might have been medical instruments. Then they looked into his ears and mouth and eyes with even stranger things. When they were finished, they took him back to the parking lot.

He didn't remember much more than that. He'd been too scared to notice anything else. Most of the time he spent yelling, except when they had some sort of gizmo stuck down his throat.

Mike Gonzo, of course, was sorry he hadn't been taken instead. He always wants to be the first to do anything new, different, or strange.

"Just think about it," he said, his blue eyes shining the way they do when he gets excited about something. "Flying around in outer space, surrounded by little green men who are poking and jabbing and probably using you for some kind of weird medical experiment."

"They weren't 'little green men,'" Laurie said. Laurie's my sister, and she's very literal. "Jimmy said they were little white *creatures*,

2

sort of the color of the Pillsbury Doughboy, and they were bald, and they had big black eyes."

"I don't care what they looked like," the Big T said. He put his index finger on the bridge of his glasses and pushed them up on his nose. "I don't want to have anything to do with any kind of spacemen."

He was looking at Mike when he said it, because Mike is just the kind of guy to get involved with little men—or creatures—from outer space, no matter what color they might be. He'd already gotten us tangled up with some sewer monsters and an invisible man, and UFOs would be right up his alley.

Mike, the Big T, Laurie, and I were sitting on the grass in the shade of a big oak tree in Mike's backyard, discussing Jimmy's story. The sun was shining, and it was a hot day, but there was a slight breeze that rustled the leaves over our heads. We were pretty comfortable in the shade.

"What about you, Bob?" Mike asked me. "Wouldn't you like to zip around the stratosphere in a flying saucer?"

I said that I wasn't so sure.

"Come on, use your imagination," Mike

prodded. "It'd be just like *Star Trek!* We could look out and see the stars!"

"I can see the stars from right here," the Big T said. "Or I could if it was night and this tree weren't in the way. They probably wouldn't look any different from a spaceship."

"Yes, they would, Geoffrey," Laurie said. She always called the Big T by his real name. We called him the Big T for obvious reasons. "There wouldn't be any pollution in the air up there, because there isn't any air. And there wouldn't be any other lights, so the stars would be much brighter."

The Big T didn't look convinced. "I'm happy just to look at them from here," he said. "Anyway, Jimmy Terwilliger probably made the whole thing up."

That was something to think about. Jimmy wasn't exactly the most truthful person in Midgeville Junior High. I think he once told me that his grandfather was an astronaut, but I don't remember an astronaut named Terwilliger.

"I don't think he made the spaceship up," Mike said. "Remember, the grounds keepers saw something, too, even if they weren't quite sure what it was. I think there's really some-thing out there, something that's looking for earthlings to examine."

"I don't think so," Laurie told him. "The government wouldn't allow it."

"Ha!" Mike said. "Do you ever watch *The X-Files?*" He pointed at the TV show's emblem on his T-shirt. "What about *Sightings?* Or *Encounters?*"

Laurie brushed back her hair and sniffed. "I don't watch things like that. I'd rather read."

I'd rather read, too, but I have to admit that I've watched *The X-Files* once or twice. I sort of like Agent Scully.

"Well," Mike said, as if he was worried about Laurie's ignorance, "if you ever watched TV, you'd know that there are things out there that no one understands and that the government can't do anything about."

"*The X-Files* isn't real," the Big T said. "It's just a TV show. It's fiction, like those books Laurie reads."

"Sometimes I read nonfiction," Laurie said.

"Then you should know about what hap-pened right here in Texas in 1957," Mike said. "There was a huge UFO that flew over Levelland. Nine or ten people saw it. It was over two hundred feet long, and every time it flew over a car, the car's engine died."

"I don't believe that," Laurie said. "And I don't believe that Jimmy Terwilliger was kidnapped by any UFO, either."

"He was on TV," Mike pointed out.

The Big T suddenly got interested. "He was?" The Big T had been on TV himself once, after our encounter with the sewer monsters. He had enjoyed the experience.

"That's right," Mike said. "I'll bet that if we saw the UFO, we'd get on TV, too."

I thought he was being pretty sneaky, trying to appeal to the Big T that way, but the Big T wasn't fooled. "No thanks," he said. "I don't mind watching spaceships at the movies or on TV, but I'm not going out looking for one around here."

Mike eyed the Big T, and then me. "I never thought you two would pass up a chance at an adventure," he said. His eyes were shining, and his red hair was bristling. "At least you could go over to Jimmy's house with me and talk to him about it."

I didn't see the harm in that, which shows

how much I know. Anyway, I said I'd go see Jimmy with Mike.

"What about you?" Mike asked the Big T.

The Big T thought about it for a long time, picking up a little acorn and rolling it around in the palm of his hand with his fingers. "All right," he said finally. "I guess I'll go."

We stood up and brushed the grass off the seats of our baggy shorts.

"What about me?" Laurie asked. "Am I invited?"

Mike gave me a "she's your sister, you handle it" look.

"You could always go home and drink some lemonade," I told her.

"Ha!" she said. "If you go see Jimmy Terwilliger, I'm coming with you."

And, of course, she did.

Chapter 2

Welcome to Earth

We didn't get to see Jimmy, though. We couldn't get to him because his house was almost completely surrounded by cars and vans and trucks.

The cars all had signs on the sides saying things like KYKR-TV Eyewitness News Team on the Go! So did the vans. The trucks were flatbeds with cameras set up on them; the camera crews were trying to look busy, even though they weren't filming anything.

Jimmy's house looked deserted. All the curtains were drawn and the garage doors were closed tight.

"Do you think he's in there?" the Big T asked.

"Sure he is," Mike said. "Those TV people wouldn't be here if he weren't at home. They're just waiting for him to come out."

"I wonder if they'd like to hear about how I saved Midgeville from an invisible man," the Big T said, looking toward a car full of reporters.

"I don't think so, Geoffrey," Laurie told him. "In the first place, the invisible man wasn't much of a threat. In the second place, the rest of us did just as much as you did."

"And in the third place," I said, "we aren't going to tell anyone about that."

The Big T shrugged. "Okay, but I'll bet they'd like to hear about it."

"Not right now, they wouldn't," Mike said. "Someone's coming out of the house."

We all looked at the house as the front door swung open. A tall, skinny man, who was probably Jimmy's dad, stepped through it.

The camera crews hopped to their cameras. News reporters were jumping out of their cars and waving their hands. They were all yelling at once.

"Over here, Mr. Terwilliger!"

"No, over here! Over here!"

"What about your son? Is he going to give us a statement?"

Mr. Terwilliger stood on the porch with his mouth shut and his arms crossed until all the yelling died down. When it finally got almost quiet, he said, "My son is not going to be giving any further statements. He doesn't feel like talking anymore about what happened. He's tired, and he can't be bothered. That's all I have to say."

He turned around and went back through the door. We could see that the news people were disappointed, and a few of them gave up and left. Most of them stayed where they were, though. They weren't going to give up so easily.

"Do you think we could sneak around to the back and get in?" Laurie asked.

"We don't want to do that," Mike said. "Jimmy has enough trouble without us bothering him."

The Big T let out a sigh of relief. "Why don't we go over to my house and play a game of croquet?"

Mike shook his head. "I've got a better idea."

"I was afraid of that," the Big T said. "I'm not sure I want to hear it."

"It's not so bad. I thought we might go over to see what Dr. Whistler thinks about all this."

Even the Big T couldn't object to that. Dr. Whitney Whistler had been a source of trouble to us when he was invisible, but he had destroyed his invisibility formula and promised not to make any more. It had a bad side effect, and besides, some not-so-nice people were trying to take it away from him.

After we'd helped Dr. Whistler out, we took on the job of keeping his lawn. He needed someone to mow and edge and rake, and we needed the money. It was a pretty good arrangement, and we'd gotten to like Dr. Whistler a lot.

"We might as well go and see him," I said. "We have to mow his lawn later this week anyway. We'll check it out, see how much it's grown."

"All right," the Big T said. "As long as there aren't any flying saucers involved."

"Don't be silly, Geoffrey," Laurie said. "They don't come around in broad daylight, do they?"

"Sometimes they do," Mike said. "But not often. Let's go."

We left the TV reporters behind and walked to Dr. Whistler's house, which sat on top of the only hill in Midgeville. The lawn looked pretty good, if I do say so myself. That is, except for something at the top of the hill, near the house.

"What's that?" Mike asked.

No one knew. We couldn't see it very well from where we were, about halfway up the driveway that led to the top. It looked as if something had happened to a big area of the grass, which was brown and dead-looking.

"I hope we don't get blamed for it, whatever it is," the Big T said. "I don't think we did anything that could cause something like that."

"We didn't," I said. "We've been very careful."

And we had been. When we got to the house, we could see that the dead grass was strictly Dr. Whitney's responsibility. In fact, it wasn't even dead. There was just a large, brown circle painted on it. There were words painted on the circle with white paint, but the letters were so big that it was hard to read them.

"I'll bet we could read them if we were looking down from the second story of the house," Laurie said.

The Big T took a deep breath. "Oh, no," he said.

"What?" Laurie asked. "What?"

"I think he's managed to read what the letters say after all," I told her.

"Well? Tell the rest of us," she said.

Mike had figured out the message, too. He spoke up first: " 'Welcome to Earth, Spacemen. Please land here.' "

"That does it for me," the Big T said. "I'm going home now. I'm gonna roll out of here like a big wheel in a Georgia cotton field."

He turned and started down the hill just as Dr. Whistler opened his front door. "Hello, everyone," he called.

Darling, Dr. Whistler's dog, came around from behind him and charged down the steps. She ran right to Laurie, who reached down and rubbed her head. Darling had once been invisible, too, but she was easy to see now. She

13

looked a little like a miniature Lassie, and she wriggled all over as Laurie stroked her.

"She's glad to see you," Dr. Whistler said when he joined us in the yard. "And so am I. Did you see my Welcome sign?"

"We saw it, all right," the Big T said. He'd come back when he heard Dr. Whistler's voice, but he didn't look very happy about being there. "Do you think something like that will get the spacemen to stop here?"

Dr. Whistler ran a skinny hand over his spiky white hair. "Who knows? They might not even know how to read English."

"Jimmy Terwilliger couldn't understand them," Mike said. "But that might just mean they didn't want him to."

"Of course," Dr. Whistler said, putting his hands in the pockets of his old jeans. "Or they might speak French. Or Italian."

"Or Russian," Laurie added.

Dr. Whistler nodded. "Or anything at all. I think it would be fascinating to meet them."

"I don't," the Big T said.

"I can understand that," Dr. Whistler said. "But there are others who might be even more interested than I."

14

"Who?" Mike wanted to know.

Dr. Whistler looked all around his yard, then back at us. "It's awfully warm out here. Perhaps we should go inside, where it's much cooler."

He turned and started back to the house, expecting us to follow him, which we did. We'd all gotten pretty warm on the walk over. Darling ran along at Dr. Whistler's heels, looking back now and then to see if the Big T was coming.

"Well?" Mike said. "What are you waiting for?"

The Big T looked at the Welcome sign. "Flying saucers?"

"That's not funny, Geoffrey," Laurie said.

"I didn't mean it to be," he said.

Chapter 3

Intergalactic War?

Dr. Whistler didn't have air-conditioning. He said that his house wasn't designed for it and didn't need it. The rooms had high ceilings, and the windows on all sides were open wide. What little breeze there was moved the edges of the curtains.

"We'll sit in the kitchen," Dr. Whistler said. "We can have something to drink in there."

"What?" the Big T asked. He was worried about what Dr. Whistler might be cooking up in the kitchen. I thought he was being a little impolite, but Dr. Whistler just laughed.

"Don't worry," he said. "It's nothing that will alter your metabolism in the way that my invisibility potion did. I've given up that sort of thing."

The Big T looked as if he weren't sure he believed him. "I think you should give up trying to contact UFO aliens while you're at it," he said.

We sat down at the kitchen table, and Darling curled up on the floor by Laurie. Dr. Whistler opened the refrigerator and looked around in it for a second or two. Then he reached in and pulled out a bottle of dark-red liquid.

"What's that?" the Big T asked, his eyes wide. Maybe he thought it was blood.

Dr. Whistler held up the bottle. "Only cranberry juice. It's good for you."

He got some glasses out of a cabinet and poured the juice into them. When he handed me my glass, I took a swallow. The juice was cold and just a little tart.

Mike drank a big swallow and put his glass down on the table. "Why did you want us to come inside?" he asked.

"You never know who might be listening," Dr. Whistler said. "I feel safer in here."

"Safer from what?" the Big T asked.

"Spacemen," Laurie said, reaching down to

rub Darling's head. Darling's tail thumped on the floor.

"Not spacemen," Dr. Whistler said. "I'm not worried about spacemen at all. I'm worried about Len Callow."

The Big T moaned. Then he said, "Len Callow's way worse than spacemen. I thought he was still in jail."

Len Callow and three of his rough pals—Gig, Ray, and Slats—had tried to steal Dr. Whistler's invisibility formula. Their plan was to make themselves invisible and then engage in a little recreational bank robbery. We had sort of put a stop to that idea, and I was pretty sure Len Callow wasn't too pleased about our interference.

"Len wasn't in jail for very long," Dr. Whistler said. "Not even overnight. He and his friends simply paid a fine and left."

"What are they up to now?" Mike asked.

Dr. Whistler shook his head. "I'm not absolutely certain. But I think they want to capture an alien from the spacecraft that has been flying above Midgeville."

"They're welcome to all the aliens they can catch," the Big T said. "*I* sure don't want any."

"That's not the point," Mike said, his eyes beginning to get that gleam. "Just think what might happen if they caught one of the aliens and did something to him. Why, it might mean intergalactic war!"

"Argghh," the Big T said. Or that's what it sounded like to me, anyway. "I was worried about getting taken for a ride on a spaceship, and now you're talking about intergalactic war! You really know how to cheer a guy up."

"Unfortunately, Mike is correct in his assumptions," Dr. Whistler said. "In fact, it could be even worse than that."

"Then I don't want to hear about it," the Big T said.

"Why do you think they want to capture an alien?" I asked.

"I went to Big John's for breakfast today," Dr. Whistler said.

Big John's was a cafe near the movie theater. A lot of people ate breakfast there. Big John was famous for his biscuits and gravy.

"Len and his cronies happened to be in the booth behind me," Dr. Whistler continued. "I don't think they knew I was there, and I overheard a little of their conversation."

"What did they say?" Laurie asked.

"I couldn't make out all of it, but I'm nearly positive that they were talking about how much money they could make if they had an alien life-form in their possession. As I understood it, they believed that they could command huge sums from the various television networks, talk shows, and tabloid programs."

"That sounds just like them, all right," Mike said. "It's a good thing they didn't see you."

The Big T nodded vigorously in agreement.

"If you believe that they didn't see me," Dr. Whistler said, "then I've given you the wrong impression."

"Argghh," the Big T said again.

"You mean they *did* see you?" I asked.

Dr. Whistler raised a hand and waggled it in the air. "I'm not quite certain. After I realized what I was hearing, I got up very quietly and started to leave. However, my hand brushed my fork and knocked it to the floor. Naturally, that got everyone's attention."

The Big T said, "Did I mention that I didn't want to hear this?"

"Don't pay any attention to Geoffrey," Laurie told Dr. Whistler. "He's really very curious about all this."

The Big T glared at her. Laurie smiled at him, but he didn't smile back.

"At any rate," Dr. Whistler said, "when my fork dropped, Len Callow raised his head above the back of the booth and looked around the cafe. I kept my face toward the door, and he may not have seen me. But I'm afraid that he did."

"Me, too," the Big T said. "Would it help if you apologized to him for eavesdropping?"

"I don't think so," Dr. Whistler said. "It's probably too late for that. I think he plans on doing something to ensure my silence."

The Big T crossed his arms on the table and put his head on them. "I was afraid you were going to say that," he mumbled.

Chapter 4

A Brief Visit from Len Callow

Nothing would satisfy Mike Gonzo until we all agreed that we would protect Dr. Whistler from Len Callow and his ruffian friends. Even the Big T admitted that it might be a good idea. After all, we had seen before that Dr. Whistler didn't do a very good job of defending himself.

So we went home and told our parents that Dr. Whistler would be calling them to ask if we could help him with an educational scientific experiment related to the UFO that had been spotted in Midgeville.

I knew it wouldn't be smart to mention Mike Gonzo to my folks. My father thinks I let Mike talk me into doing things against my own better judgment. Of course, my father's right, but that doesn't matter. Mike can talk just about anyone into doing just about anything when he sets his mind to it.

Even without knowing that Mike was involved, my parents were a little suspicious. "What kind of experiment?" they wanted to know.

"Dr. Whistler wants to see if the UFO that abducted Jimmy Terwilliger will land in his yard," I said. "We're gong to be the witnesses."

My father laughed. He didn't believe in UFOs or aliens. "All right," he said. "I'll talk to Dr. Whistler when he calls. I don't see the harm, just as long as you don't stay out too late."

"Great," I said.

"I'm going, too," Laurie said.

"You'll have to be home by nine o'clock," my father said. "That's just about dark."

"Dr. Whistler will bring us home in his car," I said. "Can we make it ten?"

My father agreed, but only because it was summer and we wouldn't have to be getting up for school.

23

"What if a flying saucer really does land?" Laurie asked. "Can we stay a little later?"

My father laughed again, giving my mother a nudge. She didn't believe in UFOs, either.

"I don't see any harm in staying a little later if something like that happens," my mother said. "Call us, though, if you get a chance."

We said that we would, but I wasn't sure there would be a telephone on board a UFO if we got abducted. I didn't think I should mention that, however.

Nothing at all happened the first night at Dr. Whistler's, except that we saw a car and found out that the paint on Dr. Whistler's lawn glowed in the dark.

"Not only that," Dr. Whistler said, "but it's environmentally safe. I'm going to patent it as soon as I find the time."

The Big T asked what the market would be for an environmentally safe glow-in-the-dark paint.

"I don't invent things just for the money," Dr. Whistler said, sounding a little hurt. "I do it for the knowledge."

"Oh," the Big T said, as if he'd never thought of that before. Maybe he hadn't.

Mike wanted to know what Dr. Whistler's plan was, just in case the aliens did land in his yard.

"I hope to communicate with them," he said. "I'd like to assure them that Earth is a peaceful place, and that we would like their friendship."

Darling barked just about then and wagged her tail to show that she was friendly.

"What if they can't read your sign?" the Big T asked. He sounded as if he hoped they couldn't.

"Oh, dear," Dr. Whistler said. "As we were saying, that's a distinct possibility. I don't know why I didn't think of that. Perhaps they'll be curious and land anyway."

"But what if they *can't* speak English?" Laurie asked. "How will we talk to them?"

"Ah. Well, I think I have an answer for that. Why don't we go down to the basement for a moment?"

We followed him to his lab, which looked more like the science classroom at Midgeville Junior High than one of the mad scientist labs you see in old movies. Dr. Whistler went to a cabinet and brought out a thick, plastic bottle filled with a shiny gray liquid.

The Big T didn't like the looks of it. "Is that an invisibility drink?"

"Oh, no," Dr. Whistler assured him. "Far from it. This is a potion that will allow me to speak and understand any language in the world—or the universe. But it works for only a brief time."

"What about side effects?" the Big T asked— as well he might, considering what had happened the last time Dr. Whistler concocted a potion.

"It has no unpleasant side effects," Dr. Whistler said.

He looked at Mike when he said it. Mike had personally experienced the side effects of the invisibility potion. The nasty change in his personality was hard to take and, fortunately, only temporary.

"How can we be sure of that?" the Big T asked.

"Oh, I've tried it myself," Dr. Whistler said. "It didn't change my personality at all. Besides, we probably won't even have to use it."

"Unless the flying saucer lands here," Mike said, as if he were looking forward to it, which, of course, he was.

"Yes," Dr. Whistler said. "Perhaps I'd better leave this out where we can get it." He set the concoction on a table and we went back upstairs.

It was only a few minutes later that the car showed up. It drove about halfway up Dr. Whistler's drive and just sat there, its engine throbbing. We recognized the car. It belonged to Len Callow. I think all of us would rather have seen the UFO.

The car's windows were tinted and dark. We couldn't see who was inside, but we all knew. After a few minutes, the car backed down the hill and drove away.

"I wish they'd come on up for a little talk," Mike said. "We could have asked them how they liked it in jail."

"*You* might want to ask them that," the Big T said. "I don't."

Mike smiled. "Maybe they'll come back."

But they didn't, and at ten o'clock Dr. Whistler took us home.

We found out the next morning that people

all around Midgeville had sighted the UFO that night, twenty-seven people, to be exact, according to the morning newspaper.

"It's still out there," Mike Gonzo said when he and the Big T came over. "We still have a chance to see it. Or to get abducted."

The Big T didn't show the same eagerness. "I hope it flies somewhere else. Like China. I think a UFO would be a big hit in China."

"You don't know a single thing about China," Laurie said.

"I know one thing," the Big T said. "I know the Chinese would like seeing that UFO better than I would."

"*Anybody* would like it better than you," Laurie said.

The Big T grinned. "Now you're getting the idea."

Chapter 5

A Close Encounter of the Gonzo Kind

The flying saucer didn't go to China, however. It showed up at Dr. Whistler's house the next night at just about ten o'clock.

It had been a quiet evening up until then. We played Monopoly and drank cranberry juice until Mike Gonzo had monopolized nearly everything, and then we sat out on the porch and watched the sky.

We saw a few skimpy clouds, and the moon, which was full and yellow. We saw a few stars, too, but for a long time there was no sign of anything like a flying saucer.

We were just about to give up and go home when we saw it.

It came gliding over the top of Dr. Whistler's house like a ghostly galleon and blocked out the moon. There was a circle of light around the bottom of the saucer, but other than that it was entirely black—blacker than the night sky. So black that it almost appeared to suck up all the light from the entire neighborhood.

It hovered silently over the lawn for what seemed like a very long time.

"They're reading the sign!" Mike said. "They're going to land!"

The Big T looked longingly down the hill. "I think I forgot to do my homework," he said. "I guess I'd better be going."

"It's summer," Laurie reminded him. "You don't have any homework."

"It's homework that I forgot to do last February," the Big T said. "It's a little late to be doing it now, I know, but better late than never."

The saucer made a funny noise, like someone coughing. It dipped to one side and began drifting away. Darling started barking and running in circles. She stood on her hind legs and pawed at the sky.

"There's something wrong with the saucer," Mike said. "They aren't going to land here."

I wasn't sure whether he was right, but the saucer sank lower and lower as it floated away from us.

"It's headed for Connor's field," Mike said. "Let's go!" He jumped off the porch and hit the ground at a dead run. Darling was right at his heels, barking excitedly.

"Wait!" Dr. Whistler called to both of them, but it was too late. Mike and the dog kept right on going. Either they didn't hear him or they ignored him. Knowing Mike, I suspected the latter.

None of the rest of us had moved. Dr. Whistler looked at us and said, "Oh, dear. I suppose we should go after him."

"Let's go then," the Big T said.

He's always complaining about how dangerous things are, and he's always talking about how he's not going to take any risks, but that's just talk. You can always count on the Big T to help out when the trouble starts. He jumped off the porch, landing a little more heavily than Mike had, and lumbered across the yard.

I followed him, stopping only to turn my

head and tell Laurie that she'd better stay right there.

"No way," she said as she raced past me, her arms pumping.

I shut up and ran after her. Connor's field was a good half mile away, and the others had a head start.

Dr. Whistler didn't come along for a while, but he caught up with me before I'd gone very far. He had long legs, and he lifted his knees high as he ran. "I do hope . . . that the ship . . . won't crash," he panted.

I was afraid that it might. It was moving very slowly and wobbling from side to side. I wondered if it would explode when it hit the ground. I hoped that, if it did, it wouldn't blow us up with it.

We must have made a funny sight as we ran—four kids, a dog, and a grown man charging through a grassy field in the moonlight, with our shadows keeping pace right beside us.

Dr. Whistler's house was at the edge of town, and the saucer was headed for the open countryside. We ran through tall grass that swished against our legs and over soft ground that squished under our feet.

Mike was still ahead of us. I could see his head bobbing up and down as he ran. I couldn't see Darling, but I could hear her barking somewhere in the distance. She had passed Mike quickly, and she was still running toward the saucer.

"What about . . . the cemetery?" Dr. Whistler asked.

Connor's field, where the saucer was headed, was a large, open area the size of three or four football fields. It wasn't fenced, and sometimes kids would go on treasure hunts there during the daytime, or maybe look for Indian arrowheads.

Nobody ever found anything, as far as I know, and no one ever went there after dark. There were lots of funny stories about Connor's field, probably because it was right next to the Midgeville Memorial Cemetery, which was directly in our path.

Surrounding the cemetery was a black wrought-iron fence, and the gates were always locked at 8:00 P.M. in the summer. There was no way through the fence, and it would take quite a while to go all the way around it.

If we went around it. A little thing like a

fence didn't bother Mike Gonzo. It didn't even slow him down. He just started climbing.

"Look," I told Dr. Whistler, pointing at Mike. "We'll have to go over."

Dr. Whistler didn't answer, but I could tell he didn't much like the idea. He was a lot older than we were.

It took us only a few minutes to get to the fence. The Big T was already there, with Laurie standing beside him. In the cemetery, Mike was zigzagging his way through the tombstones.

The Big T looked up at the top of the fence. It was much higher than his head. "It would be trespassing to go over that fence," he said. "We might get arrested."

"Mike went over," Laurie pointed out. "And no one arrested *him*."

"Yet," the Big T said.

Dr. Whistler didn't think he could make the climb. "I'll have to go around. Where's Darling?"

"She went around, too," Laurie said. "Listen."

We listened, and we could hear Darling's

34

bark off to the right, above the faint coughing sound that the saucer was making.

"I'll follow Darling," Dr. Whistler said. "All of you, promise to wait for me if you get to the saucer first."

We nodded, and Laurie started over the fence. She could climb pretty well for a girl.

I looked at the Big T. "Well?"

"Oh, all right." He took his glasses off and handed them to me. "Hold these."

"Sure," I said.

He made a jump for the fence and heaved himself up and over, landing lightly on the other side. For a big guy, he actually had some pretty good moves.

I passed his glasses to him through the bars of the fence and started climbing. The iron was still warm from the day's sunshine. I landed on the ground beside the Big T and Laurie. No one said a word as we started jogging through the cemetery.

The moon shadows wavered and shook as we ran through them. The tombstones seemed to glow with an eerie light, almost like the sign in Dr. Whistler's yard.

35

"I wish I were somewhere doing my home-work," the Big T said.

"Don't worry about your homework," Laurie told him. "If the aliens use you for some kind of hideous medical experiment, you'll never have to do homework again."

"Thanks," the Big T said. "That's a real comfort."

I wasn't really listening to them. I was look-ing for Mike. I saw him emerge from the tomb-stones and climb the fence on the far side of the cemetery.

When he got to the top of the fence, he didn't drop over to the other side. He balanced where he was, holding himself above the spikes that topped the wrought iron, looking at something.

Or looking *for* something.

It was only then that I realized I couldn't hear the flying saucer any longer.

I couldn't see it, either.

It was gone.

Chapter 6

Company's Coming

It wasn't really gone, of course. It was just out of sight in the tall grass, having settled to rest in Connor's field. It hadn't made a sound when it went down.

Mike was still poised at the top of the fence when Laurie, the Big T, and I got there.

"What are you waiting for?" the Big T asked.

"Come up here where you can see," Mike said, and we all climbed up the fence.

When we got to the top, we discovered that the saucer was very well hidden. It was so black that it seemed to blend in with the night and the darkness. It would have been very hard to spot if it flew by, high overhead, on a dark and moonless night.

The spaceship was also big, bigger than I'd thought when it first sailed overhead. It was as big as a circus tent, but not nearly as tall—more like an enormous Frisbee.

All its lights had been turned off, and it sat there, motionless and silent. If we hadn't known it was there, we might not have seen it.

The Big T looked things over and said, "Pretty good camouflage."

"Right," Mike said. "Let's take a closer look."

"I can see pretty well from right here," the Big T told him.

Mike laughed and dropped off the fence. The rest of us followed him, even the Big T. We walked through the tall grass toward the saucer just as Darling came running up, still barking. When we came to a halt, a safe distance from the saucer, she sat down by us and looked at it, too. She made a low, rumbling growl in her throat.

I looked in the direction she'd come from and saw Dr. Whistler galloping along, still getting his knees higher than you'd think he could.

And I saw something else.

I saw the headlights of a car.

"I think we've got company," I said.

Mike looked at the headlights and said, "I was hoping no one else would show up. The saucer was awfully quiet. I didn't think anyone could have heard it."

"They might have seen the lights," Laurie said.

"Or they might have been lurking around Dr. Whistler's house, waiting for it to show up," the Big T said. "And if they were, you know whose car that is."

Laurie didn't remember. "Whose?" she asked.

The Big T just looked at her.

"Oh," she said, catching on after a couple of seconds. "It's that Len Callow."

"And his thugs," Mike said as Dr. Whistler came loping up.

Dr. Whistler took a handkerchief from his back pocket and wiped his forehead. When he was through, he folded the handkerchief neatly and put it back in his pocket. There was something else bulging in his pocket, but I couldn't see what it was. He just stood there for a minute, trying to get his breath, while we watched

Len Callow's car plowing toward us through Connor's field.

"Maybe they'll get stuck in the mud," Laurie said.

"Guys like that never get stuck in the mud," the Big T said. "Trust me. Besides, there's no mud."

"Who are we . . . discussing?" Dr. Whistler asked. He wasn't gasping quite as much as he had been.

We didn't bother to answer him. We just pointed to the headlights that seemed to be bouncing up and down through the rough field like two yellow basketballs.

"Oh, dear," Dr. Whistler said.

Mike agreed. "Just what we needed."

"Rowrrf," said Darling. She didn't like Len Callow any better than we did.

We didn't have time to worry about Len Callow, however, because something else got our attention. There was a soft swooshing noise from the saucer, and we all turned to look.

A door opened in the saucer's smooth, black side, and a set of steps slid out onto the ground, landing with a light thud.

There was a soft glow from inside, and we

could see the dark silhouette of someone—or something—standing in the doorway.

"It's a space alien!" the Big T screeched.

"We don't know that," Laurie said, brushing back her hair so that she could see better. "Maybe Steven Spielberg is making a movie somewhere around here."

"Sure he is," the Big T said. "And nobody knew a thing about it. Now why didn't I think of that?"

"There's only one way to find out for sure," Mike said. He started to walk toward the saucer.

Naturally, I followed him. I don't know why I did it. I knew I shouldn't, and he hadn't even asked me to. Maybe it was just that I wasn't going to let Mike Gonzo go into outer space without me.

Darling wasn't, either. She shot past both of us and, without bothering to take the steps, she launched herself through the open door.

I didn't look back to see if anyone else was coming, even when I heard a car door slam. I knew that wasn't good news, and I started to run.

I caught up with Mike at the doorway. The

41

person or thing that had been standing in the doorway was no longer there, and there was no sign of Darling. I thought I could hear the echo of a bark somewhere inside the saucer, but I wasn't sure.

Behind us I heard a lot of yelling, and this time I looked back to see what was happening. Len Callow and his pals were trying to get past Laurie and Dr. Whistler.

Slats, the biggest of the four, was doing his best to slug Dr. Whistler, who kept twitching his head just out of reach.

Laurie had somehow managed to climb up on Gig's back; she was pulling his hair with her right hand while keeping a pretty good chokehold on his neck with her left arm.

Len Callow and Ray were chasing the Big T in our direction, but they weren't going to catch him. The Big T looked awkward and he played lineman for the Midgeville Junior High Musk-oxen, but his size and appearance were deceptive. He could outrun some of the members of the offensive backfield.

"If we're going inside, we'd better do it now," Mike whispered, peering through the doorway. "What do you think?"

"If you're going, I'm going."

"I'm going," he said, taking the steps two at a time and disappearing inside.

I hated to leave Laurie at the mercy of Gig and Slats, but she seemed to be taking good care of herself.

Chills ran down my arms as I followed Mike Gonzo up the steps and into the flying saucer.

Chapter 7

Up, Up, and Away

Once upon a time, Midgeville had been a quiet little town, probably not a whole lot different from any other little town anywhere in the country. Not very much happened there, or not very much that was exciting. We went to school, we played games, we read books, we watched a little TV.

And then, one day, something happened. Mike Gonzo led me and Laurie and the Big T down into a storm drain, and we ran into a sewer monster.

Okay, so we weren't actually *in* a sewer, and it wasn't a *real* monster. It was close enough, though, and after that the things that happened to the four of us just got stranger.

Nothing that had happened so far, however, had been quite so strange as finding myself on the inside of a flying saucer.

I was standing in what seemed to be a narrow, white hallway with a low, white ceiling. The floor was white, too, but it wasn't hard like all the other floors I've stood on before. It wasn't soft, either, but there was a little mushiness to it, almost as if I were walking on some kind of rubber.

The light inside the spaceship was dim and cool. I couldn't tell where it was coming from. There were no light bulbs or fluorescent tubes in sight. Maybe the light was coming from the walls themselves; maybe they were coated with something like Dr. Whistler's glow-in-the-dark paint.

I couldn't see Mike anywhere. I knew he had to be nearby, probably just a little farther into the saucer than I was, but all I could see was the empty hallway. There weren't even any shadows.

I heard a soft noise at my back, and I turned around so fast that my neck popped.

The steps were sliding back into the ship.

"Hold it!" the Big T yelled from just outside.

45

The steps clicked into place. Then the door began to close, but there wasn't anything I could do to stop it. There was no control panel, or if there was, I couldn't see it. There was no button to push, and there was no door handle to grab.

The Big T catapulted himself through the air, flattening out like a diver. He came sailing through the door, trying to balance something in his right hand. It was one of Dr. Whistler's flasks. He didn't drop it, but his glasses came off and bounced down the hallway. They didn't make a sound.

Just as he started to get up, there was a chuffing noise, and the whole saucer shook under us. The floor shuddered, and the saucer rose a foot or two into the air.

I could hear Len Callow yelling. "Stop right there!" he said, but of course the ship didn't stop. It kept right on going up.

There was a thump as Callow jumped into the doorway. He wasn't quite as nimble as the Big T, or maybe it was just because the ship was farther off the ground; at any rate, he didn't make it quite all the way inside. He was about halfway in and halfway out, with his legs dangling down. He clawed at the floor with his fingertips, but he couldn't get a secure grip.

I didn't see any reason to give him any help. He certainly wouldn't have helped me if I'd been in his place.

"Hello, Mr. Callow," I said.

His pasty face looked up at me. I could tell he didn't like me much. "Help me out here," he growled.

He was trying to sound friendly, but somehow it didn't quite come out that way. I'm not sure he knew what the word *friendly* really meant.

"I'm gonna fall if you don't help me," he said.

The door had stopped closing when it touched Len's arms. I wondered if the saucer could fly with an open door. I figured it could, since we were still rising very slowly.

"We're only about ten feet off the ground," I said. "The fall won't hurt you much."

The Big T got to his feet and walked down the hall for his glasses, stuffing the flask in the pocket of his shorts as he went. He picked up his glasses, put them on, and came back to where I was standing. Neither one of us knew exactly what to do. We'd never been faced with a situation quite like it.

"Should we kick him out?" the Big T asked.

I wondered what Mike would have done. I was thinking it over when Len Callow screamed.

"Yeeeeeeee!" he howled as he began to slide rapidly backward.

I walked over to the doorway to see what was happening. We were still not more than twelve feet above the ground.

Ray had apparently jumped for the opening, though why he thought he could jump that high, I'll never know.

Naturally, he hadn't made it, and to keep himself from falling to the ground, he had grabbed Len around the waist and dragged him nearly out of the saucer.

Ray had a shaved head that was nearly round and looked a little like a bowling ball sitting on his shoulders. He was looking right up at me with wide eyes.

Len was clinging to the doorsill by his fingertips. He was gritting his teeth with the effort of holding on.

"I think you should both let go," I told them. "Before it's too late."

Just as I said that, the saucer gave a lurch and went straight up into the air. My stomach sank nearly to my knees.

"Yeeeeeeee!" Len Callow yelled again.

Ray was yelling, too, but I could hardly hear him.

Then the ship stopped very suddenly, and my stomach flew right up into my throat.

Ray and Len yelled again, but I wasn't interested in them. Luckily, I had been holding on to the side of the door and hadn't fallen out. I had to stand very still and close my eyes for a few seconds before I could get my breath.

When I opened my eyes, the Big T was standing beside me. He was looking out the door at the dark ground of Connor's field, which was rapidly falling away below us.

"I think it's too late for them to let go now," he said. "Unless they can fly."

Len Callow's fingers were turning white with the effort of hanging on to the edge of the doorway. Below him, Ray's legs were kicking at the empty air. I wished Mike was there.

49

"Help . . . me . . . quick," Len said through his gritted teeth.

The Big T's foot rose up off the floor and drifted above Len's right hand.

"Don't . . . you . . . dare," Len said, his teeth still clenched.

"I guess we'd better help him," I said. I didn't really *want* to help Len, but I didn't like to think about what he and Ray would look like when they hit the ground.

"Are you sure?" the Big T asked.

"I guess so."

"We're going to be sorry."

I knew he was right, but I said, "We'll be sorry if we don't, too."

"Oh, all right," he said, and he reached down for Len Callow's hand.

Chapter 8

Into the Dark

I wasn't sure we were strong enough to do the job, but the Big T didn't even seem to strain as we heaved Len Callow up into the saucer. Of course, Len was helping as much as he could, squirming along like a caterpillar once he got partway inside again.

Ray was still hanging around Len's waist, and when he reached the level of the floor, he was able to let go and grab the edges of the door. After that, he managed to pull himself the rest of the way inside. Both he and Len wiggled away from the open door, and then they lay on the floor, panting.

With the obstructions out of the way, the door slowly and quietly closed.

"I think it would be a good idea to leave these two now," the Big T said.

I agreed. If we gave Len and Ray time to recover, they wouldn't show their gratitude for the way we'd helped them. More than likely, they'd try to find a way to open the door and toss us out.

"Which way should we go?" the Big T asked.

I looked around us. The corridor led in only one direction. "Do we have any choice?" I asked.

"I don't guess so."

We started down the hallway. Again, I thought I heard Darling's bark, and hoped Mike was with her. After we'd gone a few steps, I realized for the first time that I couldn't really see the end of the corridor. That was because it didn't go in a straight line. It curved like a snake, and it was lined with doorways. Even before making the first turn, we could see open doorways to our left and right. We couldn't see the rooms that the doorways led to. They were dark inside, so dark that we could tell nothing at all about them.

It's hard to explain the feeling that I got then. We were on an alien spacecraft, flying high above the Earth, and I wasn't at all sure that we would ever get back down. I felt sort of lost and empty inside.

"Where do you think Mike is?" the Big T asked after we'd passed a couple of the doorways. He seemed to feel just fine, but maybe he was only trying to cheer me up.

I told him that I was sure Mike was doing okay. "Darling's in here somewhere, too," I added. "I could hear her barking."

We stopped for a second to listen, but there was no noise at all. I wondered how the saucer could fly so quietly.

"We'd better keep moving," the Big T said. "Len and Ray will be after us before long."

I looked back down the corridor. Len and Ray were sitting up against the wall. Len was slapping Ray on top of his bald head and yelling at him. I couldn't make out the words, but I didn't need to. I could tell that Len wasn't happy.

Neither was Ray, but he was too busy trying to cover his head to respond to whatever it was that Len was saying.

"I don't think we have to worry about those

two for a while," I told the Big T. "They seem to be having a difference of opinion."

He looked back over his shoulder and grinned. "Good. If they keep that up, they won't be thinking about you and me. Come on."

We went around the first bend in the passageway. The light was just the same, and everything was still white. And we still couldn't hear a sound.

I put out a hand and touched the wall. There was no vibration at all.

"Do you think we're moving?" the Big T asked.

"Sure. I think something was wrong, and then they stopped on our planet and fixed it. Now we're on the way somewhere."

"Where?"

I couldn't answer that one. I couldn't tell who *they* were, either, but he hadn't asked about that. I was glad he hadn't. I didn't want to think about it.

"How did you lose Mike?" the Big T asked.

"He was right in front of me, but when I came inside, the steps made a noise. Mike didn't hear them, but I stopped to see what was happening. Mike kept right on going. He can't be too far ahead of us, though."

"What if he went through one of these doorways?"

I stopped and looked at one of the open doorways and the blackness behind it. "I hope he didn't," I said.

"But what if he did?"

"How would we ever pick the right one?" I asked.

"I don't know. I thought maybe you had an idea."

I wished that he'd stop thinking like that. We walked on for a short distance. Then the Big T stopped suddenly by a doorway and I almost bumped into him.

"Do you hear something?" he asked.

I stood beside him, listening intently, and I thought I could hear the sound of a dog barking somewhere deep inside the blackness. The sound was very faint, and it might have just been my imagination.

"It could be a dog," I said.

The Big T nodded. "That's what I thought. We should probably go through that doorway."

He might have been right, but neither one of us was eager to make the first move.

For one thing, it was very dark inside the doorway. I couldn't see a single thing. It was as if the darkness were so solid we could touch it.

For another thing, I'd seen a movie once where this alien being got inside the bodies of some humans on a nearly deserted spaceship and kept bursting out through their stomachs. It wasn't a pretty sight, and I didn't want anything like that to happen to me. Maybe the Big T had seen that movie, too, or maybe not. But he wasn't in any more of a hurry to enter the room than I was.

We might have stood there for a long time if we hadn't heard Len yelling at Ray as they came down the corridor behind us.

"I don't care if you *did* think you were going to fall," Len said. "Don't you *ever* try to drag me out of a flying saucer again!"

"I didn't try to do anything like that," Ray whined. "It's just that you were in the way when I jumped, and I grabbed hold by instinct. That's what it was—instinct."

"I don't care what it was. If you ever do it again, I'll snatch you bald-headed."

The Big T and I looked at one another. Somebody had already taken care of that little chore for Len.

"Are we going to try to outrun them, or are we going inside?" I whispered.

The Big T didn't answer. He gave me another look and did one of the bravest things I'd ever seen him to.

Either that, or one of the dumbest things.

He took a deep breath, let it out slowly, and stepped inside the dark room.

Chapter 9

From Darkness to Light

As soon as the Big T crossed the threshold, the whole room lit up.

I think the sudden brightness scared the Big T as much as it scared me, but he didn't jump quite as high as I did. He's agile, but he doesn't have much of a vertical leap.

The room was full of things that looked only slightly familiar to me. There was something that might have been a bed, but it might have been a workbench instead.

Overhead was something that looked a little bit like a large light fixture, except that there was no light coming from it.

There were silvery things hanging on the

walls, and some apronlike garments hanging beside them.

I thought about the things that Jimmy Terwilliger had talked about, the things that might have been medical instruments.

"We'd better get out of here," the Big T said.

He was right. But I could hear Len more plainly than ever. He and Ray couldn't be far away.

"Where are we going?" I asked.

The Big T pointed to the wall across the room, where I saw another dark doorway. We ran to it and went through.

Behind us, the lights went off. The second room lit up around us. The things we saw in there looked even more foreign than what we had seen in the room we left. Maybe they had something to do with the ship's power supply.

Across the room was another door. We dashed for it. Darkness closed in at our backs as yet another room was filled with light. I didn't spend any time looking around because I could hear something now, for sure.

"It's Darling," I told the Big T. "Either that, or another dog that sounds just like her."

We went through another door and then another. We were getting used to the way the light came and went.

The final room we came to was already lighted. We could see Darling in the middle of the floor. She was dancing around on her hind legs and spinning in a circle, barking at the ceiling.

"What's she barking at?" the Big T asked.

"I don't know. Why don't we go in and see?"

"Because we don't know what she's barking at."

"It can't be anything very bad if we can't see it."

"It could be invisible. We've had that problem before."

"This is not the time to get cautious," I said, though I was feeling pretty cautious myself.

I guess the only reason the Big T had gone through the first door was because he was less afraid of what might be in there than he was of Len and Ray.

"Len and Ray might still be right behind us," I said.

The Big T shook his head. He wasn't going to fall for that one.

"No, they're not," he said. "If they were,

we'd have seen the lights coming on in the other rooms."

"Have you been looking behind us?"

"No," he admitted. "But we would have noticed."

"Maybe. Anyway, nothing's hurt Darling. Let's go see what the commotion's all about."

"All right," the Big T said. "After you."

I went through the doorway, wishing Mike was with me, and saw that Darling was barking up at a hole in the ceiling.

"What's in there?" the Big T called.

"Nothing," I said over Darling's barking. "Just a big hole."

That's all there was. The room was entirely empty of the kinds of things we'd seen in the other rooms we'd passed through. There was nothing to see except the hole.

"Where does it go?" the Big T wanted to know.

"I can't tell," I said. "It's just a big black circle in the ceiling."

"And that's it? Just a hole? No little green men?"

"Just me and Darling," I said.

"You're sure?"

"I'm sure."

"Then I'm coming in," the Big T said, and he did.

As soon as he stepped inside, the lights went out and the door slid shut behind him with a snaky hiss.

Once, when I was just a kid, my mother left a door to a clothes closet open, and I went inside. I decided I'd hide behind the clothes until someone came to find me.

But no one came to look for me for a long time, and I fell asleep.

My mother must have come by and closed the door, because I woke up in total darkness. For a minute or two, I couldn't remember where I was. I was hot and sweaty. While I was asleep, I'd pulled a coat off a hanger, and it had fallen on me. It had covered most of my head, so I could feel my own breath.

I felt a little like an insect must feel when it's wrapped up tight in a spider's web and can't fight its way out. I hate to admit it, but I panicked. I started trying to get the coat off me, and I got tangled up in it. At the same time, I dragged more clothes down on top of me. I was drowning in a sea of coats and sweaters.

I didn't scream or anything, but I was sweating and kicking and gasping. My mother heard me, and before too long she came and opened the door. She turned on the light and pulled the sweaters and coats off me.

I was as glad to get out of that closet as I've ever been glad about anything, and since that time I've never liked being in the dark. When the lights went out in the little room on the flying saucer, I felt as if someone had squeezed a big fist around my chest, cutting off my entire air supply.

I opened my mouth to say something, but no words came out. There was just a little squeaking noise.

Darling wasn't barking anymore.

"Are you there?" the Big T said.

"I . . . I'm right here."

I was glad I'd managed to get the words out. I didn't want the Big T to think I was scared.

"Right where?" the Big T asked.

"Here."

I reached out to see if I could touch either him or Darling, but I felt only air.

I was still feeling around when I heard a noise. At first it was just a low hum, but then it began to get louder.

"Uh-oh," the Big T said. "I don't like the sound of that."

I didn't like it either, and I liked it less and less as the pitch went higher and higher.

Darling didn't like it any more than we did. She began to howl.

I was going to tell her that everything would be all right. I didn't get a chance, though, because that's when I was sucked off my feet and right through the hole in the ceiling.

Chapter 10

Vacuum Travel

It was like being caught in a giant vacuum cleaner hose that twisted and turned and finally dumped me out on the floor of still another dark room.

I wasn't hurt when I hit the floor because it was made of that same springy material as the floors in the other rooms. In fact, I would have been just fine if the Big T hadn't landed right on top of me.

"Uffffff," I said as the air rushed out of my lungs.

The Big T rolled off me, and I got up on my hands and knees just in time for Darling to come whooshing down and land between my shoulders. She let out a sharp bark and jumped away. I tried to stand up and bumped my head into the Big T, who seemed to be crawling around in front of me.

"My glasses fell off," he said. "Help me find them."

"You couldn't see even if you had them on," I pointed out. "It's too dark."

"That doesn't matter. I feel better when I know where they are."

I ran my hands over the floor, and after a second or two I felt something.

It wasn't the Big T's glasses, however.

It was someone's foot. "Yow!" I yelled, jerking my hand away.

"What?" the Big T said. "What's going on?"

"There's someone in here!"

"Who? What? Where?"

"Over there!" I shouted.

"It's only me, guys," Mike Gonzo said. "I was wondering when you'd get here."

It was a good thing I recognized his voice. Otherwise, I might have jumped straight through the roof and into outer space.

"They'll turn the lights on soon," Mike said.

"I think they were just waiting for you to get here."

"How do you know?" the Big T asked. He was still feeling around for his glasses.

"I don't really know. But I know that they put Darling down in that room for a reason. I think maybe to get you in here."

"If that's why they did it, it worked," I said. "Who's *they*?"

"The ones who are flying this spaceship," Mike said. "I haven't actually seen them yet."

"Then how do you know they put Darling down there?"

Mike didn't answer because the lights came on. I blinked my eyes and saw that he was sitting in a big chair, sunk into its deep cushions. There were two other chairs in the room, but they were both empty.

"Here they are," the Big T said, finding his glasses and putting them on. He stared around the room, but I couldn't tell whether he liked what he saw.

Darling came over and started licking my hand.

"Don't sit in the chairs," Mike said.

"Why not?" the Big T asked. "They look comfortable to me."

Mike nodded. "They are. But if you sit in them, you can't get out."

"You're kidding," the Big T said.

Mike gave a sad little grin. "I wish I were. I thought they looked comfortable, too, and here I am. I can't get up."

The Big T was still staring at the chairs. He didn't seem pleased by the fact that there were exactly two more of them. I know *I* wasn't pleased. It seemed to be too much of a coincidence. Three of us, and three chairs. The only good news was that there wasn't a chair for Darling.

"How did you get here in the first place?" the Big T wanted to know.

"I followed Darling to the room you were just in," Mike said. "Then I got vacuumed. I think they hoped I'd try out one of the chairs, and I did."

What a surprise, I thought. I was really glad to see him, not that I'd been afraid without him or anything.

"Do you have any idea what's going on here?" I asked.

He didn't. "I have a guess, though," he said.
"What's that?"

"I think we're being taken wherever it is that this spaceship came from in the first place. I think they were on their way home and had a little problem with their propulsion system when they stopped to look at Dr. Whistler's sign."

The mention of Dr. Whistler made me think of him and Laurie. I hoped they were all right. Suddenly, having to deal with Gig and Slats didn't seem so bad. At least Laurie and Dr. Whistler weren't on their way to the end of the universe, which appeared to be our own destination.

"What about us?" the Big T asked. "What are *we* doing here?"

"They might be wondering the same thing," Mike said. "I don't think they wanted us. I think the door opened by mistake while they were doing their repairs. Maybe it was part of what was going wrong. At first, they probably didn't even know we were here."

"So why didn't they just throw us out when they found out?" the Big T asked.

"Maybe they can't. Maybe they can't stop again."

"That's great," the Big T said. "That's really great."

"Do they know Len Callow and Ray are here?" I asked.

Mike looked puzzled. "Are you sure they're here? I haven't seen them."

"Did you see us?" I asked.

"Sure. On the monitors behind you."

I turned around and saw the video monitors mounted on the walls. They were in white cabinets, but the screens looked like any other TV screen. Nothing was showing on the screens now except an empty, white corridor, which I suppose was the same corridor that the Big T and I had been walking in.

"And you didn't see Ray and Len?" I said.

"No. Just you and the Big T."

"Invisible," the Big T said. "They must be invisible."

"They don't have any of Dr. Whistler's invisibility formula," Mike pointed out. "If they did, they would have robbed every bank in Midgeville by now. Anyway, the monitors might have been tracking you two specifically."

"Okay," the Big T said. "I guess it doesn't really matter. The question is, how do we get out of here?"

Naturally he expected Mike to have an answer. For that matter, so did I. Mike always had an answer.

"First," he said, "you might try to get me out of this chair."

"Good idea," the Big T said. "Come on, Bob."

We walked over to the chair. Darling trotted along beside us. I grabbed one of Mike's hands, and the Big T took the other.

We couldn't even raise his arms from the armrests.

We were about to try again when the ship suddenly jolted and tilted sharply to the right. The Big T and I were both caught off guard, and we tumbled across the floor, stopping only when we hit the wall.

Darling maintained her balance, but she started barking gruffly. I tried to stand up, but the ship jolted again, and I slipped down to the base of the wall.

Mike was looking at the monitors.

"What's happening?" the Big T asked. "Can you see anything?"

Mike nodded. "I'm afraid so."

" 'Afraid'?" the Big T said. "Don't tell me you're afraid."

"All right, I won't tell you that I'm afraid. But I'll tell you something else."

Mike was struggling with the chair, trying to break free of its grip.

"So tell us, then," I said.

He stopped struggling and looked over at me and the Big T. "We're in *real* trouble now," he said.

Chapter 11

Real Trouble

He didn't have to tell me that we were in trouble. The ship was shaking so much that I felt as if I were in a blender.

"What's happening?" the Big T yelled. His vocal cords were vibrating along with the ship, and his voice quavered.

"I can see Ray and Len now," Mike told us. His voice was quavering, too. "They seem to be in the main control room, and they're the ones causing the problem."

"Those rats," the Big T said. "What're they doing?"

"They're wrecking the ship," Mike said.

"Good grief," the Big T said. "They're not

73

just rats. They're idiots. If they wreck the ship—"

He didn't get to finish his sentence because the ship shuddered and dipped and slammed us back into the wall. This time even Darling couldn't keep her balance, and she came tumbling toward us.

For a few seconds the wall became the floor, and Darling, the Big T, and I sprawled out on it like woozy spiders until the ship straightened.

Mike, still stuck in one place, laughed. "There are advantages to being in this chair," he said.

"Sure there are," I said, "but only if you can get out."

I started to crawl toward him. There was no use trying to stand up. The Big T came along behind me. When we got to the chair, we could see the monitors. Ray and Len were fighting some space aliens that looked pretty much the way Jimmy Terwilliger had described them: very white and hairless, with big black eyes and tight white suits of some kind of plastic-looking material.

What he hadn't mentioned was that they didn't have any ears, and their heads looked a little like triangles with round tops. The aliens didn't look exactly human, but then they didn't look like any movie aliens I'd ever seen, either.

In the background was a large panel covered with dials and switches and soft, colored lights. Every time Ray or Len crashed into it, the ship would lurch uncontrollably. Every time they tossed one of the aliens onto it, the same thing would happen.

"We've got to stop those guys," the Big T said. "If we don't, we'll all wind up as part of a big hunk of space junk."

That wasn't a very appealing prospect to any of us.

"There must be a way to get Mike out of that chair," I said. "Even if it's a trap, there has to be a release switch or something."

We looked frantically for the switch while the fight went on in the control room and the ship rocked and rolled through space.

It was Darling who came to the rescue. She stood behind the chair and barked to get our attention. I scuttled around to where she was standing, her feet planted wide apart, and I could see a small indentation in the fabric of the chair. It looked as if the toe of an alien foot might fit right in it, but I used my hand. I stuck it in the cavity and pushed down. There was a noise like someone blowing out a breath.

"Try to get up," I said, and Mike stepped out of the chair. He even managed to stay on his feet, which was more than I could do.

"All right!" the Big T said. "Now all we have to do is find the control room."

"But I don't see any doors in here," I said.

Mike pointed. "There."

I still didn't see any door, but I followed Mike as he rubber-legged across the room. Sure enough, there was a very thin line in the soft covering of the wall. It looked like the outline of a door.

"So it's a door," the Big T said from behind me. "How do we open it?"

"How did you get me out of that chair?" Mike asked.

I looked at the bottom of the wall; there was a little indentation there. It was hard to see, but it was there. I stuck in my hand and pushed. The door slid open, revealing a lighted hallway beyond.

"See," Mike said. "It's easy when you know the trick. Let's get out of here."

"Right or left?" the Big T asked.

Mike looked at Darling. "Well? What do you think?"

Darling turned right and ran off down the corridor, barking.

"What does a dog know?" the Big T asked.

"What do *we* know?" Mike answered.

That one stumped the Big T, and me, too. So we followed the dog. We didn't have any better ideas, and she'd been right about the chair.

She led us down the hallway, never looking to the left or to the right. It was hard to keep up with her, but the ship didn't seem to be trembling quite as much now.

"Maybe Ray and Len are getting tired of fighting," the Big T said.

"I just hope they're not winning," Mike said.

They were, however, as we found out when we came to the end of the corridor. It opened into the control room, and we stepped inside.

The first thing I noticed was a huge, transparent panel, through which I could see nothing but darkness and stars, like bright points of light that seemed to go on forever. It was just about the most amazing thing I'd ever seen.

Even Mike Gonzo was flabbergasted, and he stood beside me with his mouth open in wonder.

The Big T whispered, "Gosh," which just about summed it up. What else could you say?

It would have been nice to stand there and stare at outer space for a long time, but of course we couldn't. We had other things to deal with, like the fight that was going on in front of us.

Ray and Len were doing a job on the crew of the saucer. Two of the aliens lay on the floor and two others were fighting a losing battle against Len and Ray, who were bigger, stronger, and probably a whole lot meaner.

They also weren't very happy to see us.

"It's the runts from the Doc's," Ray said as he pounded one of the aliens with a hard right to the side of the head. The alien slid down the control panel and lay still.

"Right," I said. "But don't forget, we're the runts who just saved your lives."

"You saved their lives?" Mike said, as if he couldn't believe it. I didn't blame him for being skeptical. I could hardly believe it myself.

"Yeah, they saved us, and it was real nice of them," Len said, kicking the legs out from under the alien he was fighting and punching him on top of the head.

The alien fell and didn't get up.

Len smiled with satisfaction down at the alien and said, "But it was a big mistake on their part. They should've kicked us out when they had the chance. Let's get 'em, Ray."

They started toward us, their big, hairy fists swinging at the ends of their long arms. Darling growled at them, and the fur on her back stood up, but that didn't bother them at all. They walked right past her, never taking their eyes off us.

"See," the Big T said, giving me a reproachful look and shaking his head sadly. "I told you we were going to be sorry."

Chapter 12

Down We Go

"Wait a minute," Mike said to Len and Ray.

In general, I believed that he could talk anybody, even adults, into anything. But not this time. I didn't think Len and Ray would be inclined to listen.

They stopped, though, so Mike kept right on talking. "I don't know why you want to hurt us," he said. "We haven't done anything to you. Besides, you might need us."

Len thought that was funny. When he was finished laughing, he said, "We don't need anybody. We're going to take this spaceship and make a million dollars."

"Who's going to fly it?" Mike asked, as if he

knew how. I was pretty sure he *didn't* know, but he sounded convincing. He always sounded convincing.

"We can fly it," Len said. "Nothing to it. And if we can't, they can." He jerked a thumb toward the still unconscious aliens. "We'll persuade them."

"I guess you *don't* need us, then," Mike said, and started backing toward the hallway.

"No," Len said. "I guess we don't. Come on, Ray."

They came toward us again. Darling barked and jumped at them, giving me and the Big T time to follow Mike into the hallway.

"Where do we run?" the Big T asked.

"Wait for me, and then do what I do," Mike said.

Len and Ray crowded through the doorway. Ray was clenching and unclenching his fists as if he couldn't wait to hit something, preferably an honor student at Midgeville Junior High. He was smiling, too, but it wasn't a nice smile. It was the smile of a starving wolf with a fresh pork chop in its sights.

"How about if we start running now?" the Big T said.

Mike held up a hand. "Wait."

Len and Ray were only about ten feet away. Waiting wasn't easy.

When the two were way too close for comfort, Mike dropped his hand, yelled "Now!" and ran straight toward them.

They were as surprised as I was, which is why Mike was able to duck right under their grabbing arms and sprint back into the control room.

It took me and the Big T a second to catch on, but Len and Ray turned slightly as Mike went past them, so the Big T and I slipped by as well. Ray threw a punch, and his heavy fist clipped my left ear, which suddenly seemed to burn as if it were on fire. There was no other damage, however, and the Big T and I glided to a stop just inside the control room door.

"Close it!" Mike yelled.

My toe scuffed around on the wall and slipped into the slot just as Len got there. The door slid shut with a whoosh, nearly nipping off his nose.

He put out a hand to try to stop the door from closing, but all he succeeded in doing was to trap his fingers between the door and the wall.

I could hear him screaming through the tiny crack that remained. It was a thin, strained scream, so I suppose that his fingers were really hurting. I could only see the fingertips. They were twitching as if something was shooting electricity through them.

I didn't feel a bit sorry for him, considering the way my ear felt, but I guess the Big T did. "Can we get his fingers out of there?" he asked.

"You're the one who wanted to kick him and Ray out of the saucer," I reminded him. "If we get his fingers out of there, we'll just be sorry again."

The Big T nodded. "You're probably right."

We looked around for Mike, who was standing in front of what I guessed was the control panel. He was studying the knobs and dials as if he was trying to figure them out. It all seemed very confusing to me.

Darling was looking, too. She had about as much of a chance of making sense of things as I did.

The four aliens were beginning to stir a little, and one of them sat up and rubbed his head.

He made a noise that I suppose must have been a groan.

The Big T looked worried. "I hope they know we're the good guys."

"If they don't," Mike said, "we can tell them."

I wasn't so sure. I said, "What if they can't understand us?"

The Big T reached into his back pocket. "No problem. I've got Dr. Whistler's little potion." He brought out the bottle and held it up.

"Good," Mike said. "Why don't you put it down over there?"

Something that might have been a table stuck up out of the floor alongside three chairs. The chairs faced the big window that looked out into space.

"I'd like to sit down and just watch for a while," the Big T said as he looked out the window. "I've never seen anything like that before."

"I wouldn't sit in any chairs if I were you," Mike said. He was obviously thinking of the way he'd been trapped.

"Oh," the Big T said, remembering. "I guess you're right." He put the bottle on the table.

There were several small balls sticking up from the tabletop, so he set the bottle in the middle of them.

Len was still yelling outside the door, but now he was screaming at Ray, telling him to get the door open. Darling padded over and started barking at them.

I was worried that Ray might find the little slot, so I said, "Do you think they'll figure out how to get in here?"

Mike said there wasn't much we could do about it unless I knew how to lock the door, which I didn't. "So don't worry about it," he told me. "If they ever do figure it out, we'll have some help."

He looked over at the aliens, all of whom were now sitting up and gazing around the room with their big black eyes. They seemed a little dazed, but other than that they appeared to be all right.

We were all right until the Big T touched one of the balls that stuck out of the tabletop. He rolled it under his fingers like a keyboard mouse, and when he did, the spaceship made a ninety-degree turn and dived straight down at about a thousand miles an hour.

Chapter 13

Pulling the *Gppzr*

We all flew up and back and finally smashed together on the wall by the door: Darling, the four aliens, me, Mike, and the Big T.

The force of the dive held us there for a second or two, and then we all dropped to the floor and started sliding toward the big window.

Through the window we could see the earth. It would have been a beautiful sight if it hadn't been getting so much closer with every passing nanosecond.

"We're gonna die! We're gonna die!" It was Len, screaming from the corridor. I thought he was being a real coward, considering that he couldn't even see out the window.

I got a hand on one of the chairs and stopped myself from sliding. The Big T was holding on to another chair, and so was Mike.

"I hope you've learned an important lesson," Mike said.

"Don't worry," the Big T assured him. "I won't touch that thing again."

I told him I thought that was a fine idea. Then I said, "But how do we stop ourselves from crashing? At this speed, this saucer will be mashed into something about the size of a quarter."

"More like a dime," the Big T said. He tended to be gloomier about things than I was.

"Try to get us straightened out," Mike said. "I'm going to see about those guys."

The aliens had all slid into a heap against the window, where they lay still and quiet. They hadn't quite recovered from their fight with Len and Ray after all.

Darling was there with them. She must have liked them. She was licking their faces.

Mike let go of the chair and slid over to check out the aliens. The Big T said, "Who's going to try to straighten *us* out? I've already promised I wouldn't touch that ball again."

"Are you sure?" I asked.

"I'm sure. What if I sent us back in the other direction? We'd probably crash into the moon. Or maybe Jupiter."

"Okay," I said. "I'll see what I can do." I didn't want to, but I didn't have much choice. Somebody had to do it, and there wasn't anyone else left.

I inched myself over to the table, keeping a good grip on the chair. When I got to the table, I pulled myself around to where I could see the top. There were three of the little balls. Dr. Whistler's little bottle, which the Big T had put there, was long gone, of course.

"Which ball did you touch?" I asked the Big T.

In spite of all the tumbling around, he still had his glasses on. He pushed them up on his nose and said, "The one in the middle. I think I moved it forward, but I'm not sure."

He wasn't sure. Great. I stretched out my fingers.

"I might have moved it backward, though," he said.

My fingers stopped in midair. "Why don't

you give it some thought? I don't want to make a mistake and make us go faster."

While he was thinking, I looked out the window. The earth was growing larger and larger. It was a beautiful blue and white ball, and I would have enjoyed looking at it a lot more if I hadn't been afraid we might enter its atmosphere at such a high speed that we'd burn to a cinder.

Burning or crashing—neither option had much appeal for me.

"Forward," the Big T said. "I moved it forward. I'm sure."

I reached out my hand.

"But I think I touched one of the other little balls, too," he said. "When I fell."

I sighed. "Which one?"

"The one on the left. That's the one that made us go faster."

I hoped he was right. I put my hand on the ball on the left and very gently twitched it backward. The ship started to slow down almost at once.

I eased the middle ball back. We began to level out, so I kept moving it cautiously until I thought the floor was horizontal again.

After that, I felt a lot better about things and I turned to see what Mike was up to. He seemed to be talking to the aliens, one of whom was pointing to a cabinet on the opposite wall.

Mike nodded and went to the cabinet. He was opening it when I heard the door to the control room slide open.

Ray and Len came through. Len's left hand dangled at his side, and the fingers looked swollen, but he probably wouldn't need it. He and Ray most likely could have taken us all with only three hands.

"You little nerds have had it," Len said. "We're gonna break you like rotten eggs."

"I don't think so," Mike said.

He opened the cabinet and reached inside. When his hand came back into sight, he was holding a contraption that was obviously a weapon of some kind, even if it did look like a cheap plastic imitation of a Super Squirter.

"This belongs to my friends," Mike said. "Their names are Fzz, Bzz, Czz, and Wzz."

Each of the aliens nodded as his name was called. They all looked so much alike that it was hard to tell which was which.

"I don't care if their names are Eeny, Meeny, Miney, and Moe," Len said. "We're gonna take you brats apart."

"You could try," Mike said, holding up the weapon. "But if you do, I'll be forced to use this."

"That toy?" Len said. "Don't make me laugh."

"You should not laugh," said one of the aliens. I thought it might be Bzz. "The weapon will fry your *izzrp*—"

"Your gizzard," Mike said.

I could see a bottle on the floor beside him. Mike had obviously taken a sip of Dr. Whistler's potion!

"Gizzard. That is correct," the alien said. "It will fry your gizzard like cheap *trsckk*."

"Bacon," Mike said.

The alien—Bzz—spoke English very well, with hardly any accent at all. He had a little trouble with some of the words, but "gizzard" and "bacon" probably weren't all that common on his home planet.

"I don't believe that thing would fry a noodle, much less my *izzrp*," Len said.

"Gizzard, boss," Ray told him. "The little guy said it means 'gizzard.' "

"Shut up, Ray," Len told him.

Ray shut up.

"Before you do something unintelligent," Bzz said to them, "my new friend Mike will give you a demonstration."

He said something to Mike that I didn't quite hear, and then Mike asked me, "Do you have anything in your pocket that you don't mind losing, Bob?"

I reached into a pocket and pulled out a milk cap that I hadn't known was in there. It had a picture of a flying dragon on it. "There's this," I said, holding it up.

"Put it on the floor," Bzz said. "And step away from it."

I did what he said.

"Now, Mike," Bzz said. "Be sure the setting is on *frrllg.*"

Mike looked at something on the handle of the weapon. "It's on *frrllg.*"

"Very well," Bzz said. "Aim it and pull the *gppzr.*"

Mike took aim, pulled the *gppzr,* and a beam

of light leapt from the muzzle of the weapon. The milk cap flashed, smoked, and disappeared.

Darling barked happily and danced a little jig.

"That could have been your *izzrps*," Mike told Len and Ray. "Or your eyeballs. So why don't you just sit down on the floor and relax?"

Len and Ray gave it a little thought, but not much. They looked at each other, shrugged, and sat down.

But I don't think they relaxed.

Chapter 14

Two Volunteers

After all the excitement, things got back to something like normal, or to what was something like normal if you were on a flying saucer.

The idea was that we would go back to Midgeville and land in Connor's field. I hoped that Laurie and Dr. Whistler were all right and hadn't worried too much about us.

Bzz was the pilot of the saucer, and he sat in the chair next to the table in order to manipulate the steering and accelerator balls properly. He was a lot better at it than either the Big T or I had been, but of course he'd had more practice.

Len and Ray sat on the floor near the doorway, scowling at each other and everyone else, while Fzz stood near them, holding the weapon (which was called a *przzt*, by the way) so that he could fry their *izzrps* if they tried any funny business.

Czz and Wzz were looking over all the dials and making sure that things were running as they should be.

Darling was curled up on the floor, sound asleep. I wondered if she even knew that we were flying along through outer space. Probably not. And if she did, she didn't care. Dogs are like that.

Since things had calmed down, we had time to ask Bzz a few questions, such as where he had learned to speak English so well.

"We have studied your culture for the past several years by watching your Nickelodeon channel on television," he said. "We have absorbed our knowledge from all the classic programs that are presented."

"Like what?" the Big T asked. *"I Love Lucy?"*

Bzz nodded. "Certainly. 'Hey, Lucy! I'm home!' "

"Hey," the Big T said, "that's not bad. Who else can you do?"

Bzz thought for a second, then said, " 'Oh, Ro-o-o-b.' "

"Pretty good," the Big T said. "That's Laura on *The Dick Van Dyke Show,* right?"

Bzz nodded. He seemed pleased that we'd recognized his impersonation.

"Anything else?" I asked.

Bzz frowned with his small mouth. " 'Just give me the facts, ma'am. That's all I want. Just the facts.' "

"Dragnet," Mike said, with a glance at Len and Ray.

"Yes," Bzz said, noting the look. "We have seen many persons such as Len and Ray on *Dragnet.*"

"How about *Gilligan's Island?*" the Big T asked. "Have you ever seen that one?"

"Of course. We are especially fond of the episode in which they nearly get off the island but fail to do so in the end."

"Wouldn't that be just about any episode at all?" Mike asked.

"Perhaps. All are of equal excellence."

It was hard to believe that someone who

liked *Gilligan's Island* could come from a culture advanced enough to have developed space travel, but I was too polite to say so.

Instead, I said, "What I'd like to know is why you picked up Jimmy Terwilliger and did those things to him."

Bzz looked thoughtful. "I am not sure that I know who you mean. Is this Jimmy Terwilliger on television?"

Mike said, "No. He's the kid you picked up the other night for experimental purposes."

"Oh," Bzz said. "Him."

The Big T glanced around nervously, as if he thought the control room might suddenly morph into a medical lab. I felt a little nervous myself, to tell the truth, and I wished Mike were still holding the *przzt.*

"Yes," Mike said. "Him. Why did you pick him up and examine him?"

"It is something we have to do on occasion," Bzz said. "It is part of our job, but not a part that we like very much."

"Just exactly what *is* your job?" the Big T asked, as if he didn't really want to know the answer.

" 'To boldly go—' "

97

He didn't fool anybody with that one.

"Hold on," Mike interrupted. "That's not your job. That's from *Star Trek*."

"You are correct," Bzz admitted. "However, it is true of me and my crew as well. We are explorers, mainly, and exploration is what all four of us prefer. But sometimes we have to do other things to keep our superiors happy. They like getting reports on the various . . . *ysbrrs* that we encounter."

"*Ysbrrs*," the Big T said. "That would mean what, exactly?"

"Life-forms," Mike said quickly, adding, "You know, that stuff Dr. Whistler mixed up really does work well."

"It lasts longer than he thought it would, too," I said.

The Big T wanted to get back to the main topic. "I still don't like that part about examining life-forms."

"We have never harmed anyone," Bzz said, a little defensively, I thought. "Your body chemistry is much like ours, and we are merely making comparisons. We take temperatures, do a vital signs check, and that is all. Nothing that one of your doctors would not do during a routine checkup."

"How about the way you treated us?" the Big T asked. "You trapped Mike in that chair, and you vacuumed me and Bob up through the ceiling."

"You were not harmed. And it was a necessary precaution. How were we to know that you were not like the two on the floor?"

He had a point there. After all, we had more or less invaded their ship.

"What was wrong with your spaceship?" I asked. "It seemed as if you had a problem."

"We saw a sign asking us to land," Bzz said. "While we were reading it, our *hzztt* failed."

I looked at Mike. He said, "There's no word for that in English."

"It is a part of our propulsion system," Bzz explained. "We were in danger of crashing, but fortunately Wzz was able to replace the *hzztt* and allow us to be on our way. But not before we had obtained several extra passengers."

"Bob and the Big T and I wanted to see what a flying saucer was like," Mike said. "As for Len and Ray over there, I think they came aboard because they wanted to volunteer for some of your medical experiments."

Bzz gave Len and Ray a speculative look. "We do not often get volunteers," he said.

"Don't you listen to those little goobers!" Len yelled. "Nobody's going to experiment on me!"

I suppose we shouldn't have gotten him so excited. He lurched into Fzz, got both hands on the weapon that Fzz was holding, and jerked it away.

"All right," he said, waving the weapon around. "Now it's my turn to fry some *izzrps!*"

Chapter 15

A Comfortable Place to Sit

Don't worry about a thing," Mike said. "He might have the *przzt,* but he doesn't know how to use it."

"It's just like any gun," Len said. "I pull the trigger, and you get fried."

"Not exactly," Bzz said. "It is a bit more complicated than that."

"Close enough," Len said. "Now all of you go stand over by the window."

"I feel that I should warn you about one thing," Bzz said. "If you use the weapon incorrectly, *you* will be the one to fry. As will anyone who is near you."

Ray looked at the gun and at Len. Then he edged away from him.

"Don't listen to that stuff, Ray," Len said. "He doesn't know what he's talking about."

"It's *his* gun," Ray pointed out.

I saw Bzz's fingers, of which he had only four, edging toward the center ball on the little table. I braced myself for what I thought was about to happen.

"Watch it, bub," Len said, swinging the weapon toward Bzz. "I know what you're thinking."

"I do not believe that," Bzz said. "It is impossible to know what another is thinking."

"Never mind that. Just get up and get over by the window."

"Who will fly the ship?" Bzz said.

"I've been watching you," Len said. "I can handle it."

"Uh-oh," the Big T said. "This is going to be worse than I thought."

"Move it," Len told us, and we shuffled toward the window, all except Bzz.

"You, too," Len said.

"You should not pull the trigger," Bzz said. "I have warned you."

"Right. But I don't believe you. So move it."

While Len was talking to Bzz, Mike was nudging Darling with his toe. She turned her head sleepily and looked up at him.

"Bad guys," Mike whispered.

Darling's ears perked up.

"What are you saying?" Len asked.

Mike looked innocent. "Who? Me?"

"Yeah, you. I heard you."

Darling had turned to look at Len. She didn't like him, and maybe with a little encouragement, she'd do something about it.

Mike shrugged. "I didn't say anything."

"Don't mess with me," Len said, swinging the weapon from side to side.

"Go get him, Darling!" I said.

Darling leaped from the floor, landed on top of one of the chairs, and launched herself at Len.

Maybe he would have tried to shoot her if Bzz hadn't already worried him about what might happen. As it was, he didn't shoot. He just put the weapon up in front of his face as Darling crashed into him.

We were right behind her.

I sat on Len's chest, the Big T tackled Ray, and Mike grabbed the weapon.

103

"What do we do now?" I asked.

"I have an idea about that," Mike said.

That's one thing I have to say about Mike. He always has an idea.

Fzz, the Big T, Mike, and I marched Len and Ray down the hallway to the room where the Big T and I had found Mike. The chairs were still there, looking just like regular chairs.

"What's going on?" Len said. "What are you going to do with us?"

Fzz poked him in the back with the weapon, and Mike said, "Not much. I'm sure the floor was getting hard, so we're just going to give you a more comfortable place to sit."

Len eyed the chairs suspiciously. "Why are you being so nice to us?"

"Because we like you," Mike said. "Now have a seat."

They were reluctant, so Fzz poked them again.

"All right, all right," Len said. "Don't get a wedgie. We'll sit down." He walked over to one of the chairs and put his hand on it, then jerked his hand back and looked at it. Nothing had happened.

"They look like pretty comfortable chairs," Ray said.

"Shut up," Len told him. "Since you think they look so comfortable, why don't you go first?"

"Sure," Ray said, and he sat in one of the chairs.

"Well?" Len asked.

"Not bad," Ray said. He didn't try to get up, which was just as well.

Seeing that Ray was unharmed, Len sat in the other chair. As soon as he had settled himself, Fzz lowered the weapon.

It was just the moment Len had been waiting for. He lunged upward.

Well, that's not exactly true. He *tried* to lunge upward, but he didn't get anywhere. His body remained securely in the chair, although his head did bob up and down a couple of times.

"What's going on here?" he said with a puzzled look. "What have you done to us?"

"We've just made you comfortable," Mike told him.

"And it's made *us* a lot more comfortable, too," the Big T said. "Trust me."

Len didn't trust anybody. "Let me out of here!" he said, writhing around inside his clothes. It didn't do him any good. He could writhe all he wanted, but he wasn't going to be able to get out of that chair.

For a second, I wondered how the chair worked. I was sure that Dr. Whistler would have liked a chance to look at it.

Thinking of Dr. Whistler made me think again about what had been happening to him and Laurie when the saucer took off. It wasn't exactly as if I'd deserted them. I was just following Mike Gonzo, as usual, but I wasn't sure Laurie would see it that way.

"How long will it take us to get back to Earth?" I asked Fzz.

Fzz didn't speak English as well as Bzz. He said, *"Jzzpt."*

I looked at Mike, who shook his head. "The potion's worn off, I guess. I don't know what that means. But it can't be very long."

I told him that I hoped not. "I'm worried about Dr. Whistler and Laurie."

The Big T said, "Ha! You'd better worry

about Gig and Slats. Laurie's meaner than they are."

"I'm not so sure about that," I said.

"Wait and see," the Big T said. "She'll have them begging for mercy."

"I hope so," I said.

Chapter 16

Good-bye to the Saucer

The saucer touched down in Connor's field without making a sound and settled gently onto the grass. Bzz walked with us to the door, which slid open at a voice command. The steps clicked down to the ground.

We really hadn't been gone as long as it had seemed, probably not more than an hour, though a lot had happened in that time. It was still dark in the field. I didn't see Len's car, and there was no sign of Laurie and Dr. Whistler.

Darling bounded past us and down the steps, barking happily. I thought that she was just glad to be back on Earth, but then I heard Laurie calling her and felt a lot better about things.

"Meeting you has been an interesting experience," Bzz said to us. "Perhaps someday we will meet again."

"Are you going to hang around here much longer?" the Big T asked.

"No. The fact that you have seen and talked to us now makes it impossible for us to remain in your solar system. We are not yet ready to be featured in your newspapers and television reports."

"We won't tell anyone what happened," Mike said. "We're not like Len and Ray."

"I am sure that is true, but I am also sure that Len and Ray will tell everyone they meet."

"No one will believe them, though," Mike said. "They aren't exactly respectable citizens."

"I hope that you are correct. And I wish to thank you for suggesting that they 'volunteer' for our medical analysis. I promise you that they will not be harmed."

"Hey, you can harm them," the Big T said. "We won't mind."

Bzz did something with his mouth that might have been a smile, but it was hard to tell. "Later," he said, "we will return and re-lease them here."

"Could you release them somewhere else?" the Big T asked. "Like in the middle of the Gulf of Mexico?"

Bzz smiled again. "As I told you, we have never harmed anyone. This would not be a good time to start, not even with your friends Len and Ray."

"They aren't our friends," the Big T said.

"I know. I was attempting to make what you call a joke."

We all smiled, and then I heard Darling again. She was leading Laurie and Dr. Whistler across the field toward us.

"I believe that I should leave now," Bzz said. "As interesting as our encounter has been, I do not think it would be a good idea to meet any-one else just now."

"Dr. Whistler will be really disappointed," I said. "He's the one who made the sign."

"It was a very nice sign," Bzz said. "But we are not yet ready to establish full contact with your planet."

"All right," Mike said. He started down the

steps. "But you'll let us know if you're ever in the neighborhood again, won't you?"

"If it is possible, we will do so. We would like to examine your *krzzq* more carefully."

"I think he means Darling," Mike said. "I'm not sure she'd like that, Bzz."

"Perhaps if you explained it to her. . . ."

We had reached the bottom of the steps and turned to look back.

"I'll see what I can do," Mike said. "Dr. Whistler's drink worked on your language. Maybe it'll work with dogs, too."

"I hope so," Bzz said, "Now thank you, and good-bye."

We said good-bye, and the steps slid back into the ship, clickety-click. The door closed as soon as they disappeared.

"Oh, dear," Dr. Whistler said behind me. "I was hoping that I might be invited inside."

"No," Mike said. "The pilot's in a little bit of a hurry."

"Oh, drat. I'm sure there was a lot to be learned from them."

The Big T nodded. "You can say that again."

"What about Gig and Slats?" I asked, to change the subject.

"They left," Laurie said.

"It was truly amazing," Dr. Whistler said. "In fact, I never saw anything quite like it."

"Like what?" I asked.

Dr. Whistler shook his head as if he couldn't believe even the memory of what had happened. "Your sister," he said. "She's quite a fighter."

"She's been taking a self-defense class," I said.

The Big T looked at her with something like respect. "No kidding?"

"That's right," Laurie said. "You'd better be nice to me from now on, Geoffrey."

The Big T opened his mouth to answer, but he didn't get a chance. The saucer lifted off the ground and rose high above us.

Darling barked good-bye, and the rest of us waved, though I'm not sure Bzz or the others could see us. For a few seconds the saucer just hung in the sky. Then it waggled from left to right as if to signal that everything was just fine. Before we could blink, it soared straight up and out of sight.

I think we were all sorry to see it go, even the Big T, who would never have admitted it.

After a second or two, we started walking toward the cemetery fence, with Darling dancing along beside us.

"What about Len and Ray?" Dr. Whistler asked after we'd gone a little way. "Are they still aboard the saucer?"

"Yes," Mike said, "but I wouldn't be jealous of them if I were you. We'll tell you all about it when we get back to your house. Your potion worked great, by the way."

"Wonderful! Did you bring back what was left?"

Mike patted his pockets. They were all empty. "I guess I must have left it on the ship."

"Oh, well. I can make some more if I ever need it."

"They liked your sign, though," I said.

He smiled at that. I knew it would cheer him up.

"I wish I could have gone with you," Laurie said.

"Dr. Whistler needed your help," Mike told her.

"That's true," Dr. Whistler agreed. "Though I believe I gave a rather good account of myself."

"He kicked them in the shins," Laurie said. "And I pulled Gig's hair. He didn't like that very much. I think he was even crying a little."

"They were really rather cowardly without Len to give them their orders," Dr. Whistler said. "They left in quite a hurry."

"Len would be upset if he knew they'd taken his car," Mike said.

The Big T looked up into the sky. "I'll bet he's upset enough right now without having his car to worry about."

He was probably right about that.

When we came to the fence, Dr. Whistler said, "I think we should just walk around it."

We all agreed with him. There was no need for climbing now.

We got back to the house and went in for a glass of cranberry juice. Dr. Whistler said that he would call our parents before we told our story. He wanted to let them know we were all right, so they wouldn't worry.

"Tell them that we got involved in a Monopoly game," Mike said. "I don't think they'd believe it if you told them the truth."

While he went to make the calls, we sat out on the porch and sipped our juice. Darling lay down beside us. Now and then we would look up at the sky, but, of course, there was nothing up there except the moon and the stars.

Once, for just a second, something like a shadow passed across the face of the moon.

"Do you think that could be them?" the Big T asked.

"No," I said. "It was just a cloud."

"Maybe," Mike said.

We didn't talk for a while. Then the Big T said, "Jimmy Terwilliger got on TV when he told about being picked up by a saucer. I wonder if those reporters would like to hear how I prevented an intergalactic war and saved the world by taking care of Len and Ray for the saucer men?"

He was stretching the facts a little, but then he did that almost every time we got involved in an adventure.

"We're not going to tell anybody about what happened," Mike said. "We owe it to Bzz to keep quiet. He's on a peaceful mission."

"Yeah, but going on TV—"

"If you say anything, Geoffrey, I'll use my self-defense skills on you," Laurie told him.

"Oh, wow, I'm shaking."

"You'd better be."

The Big T didn't bother to say anything after that, and we were all quiet for a while. We could hear Dr. Whistler talking on the phone, and occasionally Darling's tail would scuff along the floor as she wagged it.

I don't know what the others were thinking, but I was thinking about what an amazing thing had happened to us. And, of course, I was wondering what even more amazing thing might happen next.

It might be anything. When you had a friend like Mike Gonzo, you could never be sure.

About the Author

BILL CRIDER teaches English at Alvin Community College in Alvin, Texas, and insists that neither the town nor the college was named for a singing chipmunk. Besides the books in the Mike Gonzo series, he is the author of *A Vampire Named Fred* and more than thirty mystery, Western, and horror novels for adults. He likes alligators, cats, paperback books, and old baseball cards.

R•L•STINE'S
GHOSTS OF FEAR STREET®

1 HIDE AND SHRIEK 52941-2/$3.99
2 WHO'S BEEN SLEEPING IN MY GRAVE? 52942-0/$3.99
3 THE ATTACK OF THE AQUA APES 52943-9/$3.99
4 NIGHTMARE IN 3-D 52944-7/$3.99
5 STAY AWAY FROM THE TREE HOUSE 52945-5/$3.99
6 EYE OF THE FORTUNETELLER 52946-3/$3.99
7 FRIGHT KNIGHT 52947-1/$3.99
8 THE OOZE 52948-X/$3.99
9 REVENGE OF THE SHADOW PEOPLE 52949-8/$3.99
10 THE BUGMAN LIVES! 52950-1/$3.99
11 THE BOY WHO ATE FEAR STREET 00183-3/$3.99
12 NIGHT OF THE WERECAT 00184-1/$3.99
13 HOW TO BE A VAMPIRE 00185-X/$3.99
14 BODY SWITCHERS FROM OUTER SPACE 00186-8/$3.99
15 FRIGHT CHRISTMAS 00187-6/$3.99
16 DON'T EVER GET SICK AT GRANNY'S 00188-4/$3.99